A Lion Song

by Judy Ling

The little boy got out of bed.
"Today is going to be a special day,"
he said to his mother.

"And why's that?" she asked.

"Because I'm going to do
something different and exciting.
I'm going to the mountains
to catch a lion song,"
the little boy said.

"There are no lions in our mountains,"
said his mother.

"Oh yes there are!" the little boy said.

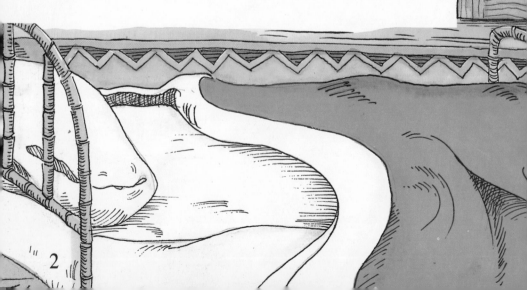

2

The little boy got some binoculars,
a jam jar with a lid, and a butterfly net.
He set off for the mountains.

On the way, he passed an old woman
sitting on a park bench.

"Where are you going this fine morning?"
the old woman asked him.

"To the mountains," said the little boy.

"That sounds like fun," said the old woman.
"What are you going to do there?"

"I'm going to catch a lion song,"
said the little boy.

"But you don't catch songs,"
said the old woman.
"You have to make them up."

"Grown-ups have to make them up,"
said the little boy, "but I know how
to catch them."

"I see!" said the old woman.
"Well, good luck, little boy.
Be sure to catch a good fierce song!"

The little boy was gone all day.
His mother was very worried about him.
It was almost dark when he came home.
He was tired, and his clothes were dirty.

"I did it, Mother!" he said.
"I caught a lion song,
just as I told you I would."

The little boy took the lid off his jam jar.
"Listen! It goes like this:"

At dead of night the lions prowl.
Listen hard. You'll hear them growl!
And when you hear the lions roar,
Shut your windows! Bolt your door!
Guard your children as they sleep
From lions in the jungle deep!

"That was a lovely song," said his mother.

"I know," said the little boy.
"Tomorrow I think I'll catch
a tiger song."

"There aren't any tigers around here,"
said his mother.
But the little boy didn't hear her.
He was fast asleep.

The next morning, the little boy
got up bright and early.
He ate his breakfast in a hurry.

"Take good care, my little boy!"
said his mother as he went out the door.
"Tigers can be fierce, you know."

The little boy smiled to himself
and set off.

He hurried to the market place.
He went to the bird shop.
There were birds everywhere.
Bamboo cages hung from the rafters
and were stacked high all over the floor.
There were big birds, little birds,
birds of all colors and sizes.

"What can I do for you?"
asked the bird seller.

"I want a bird," said the little boy.
"Not just any old bird.
It's for my mother.
Today's her birthday, you see."

The bird seller showed him bird after bird.
The little boy shook his head at each one.
They were all too ordinary.

"I'm afraid I can't help you,"
said the bird seller.

13

The little boy walked through the park, wondering what to do. The old woman was there again, on the park bench.

"You look sad, little boy," she said. "What's the matter? Didn't you catch your lion song?"

"Yes, I caught my lion song, and it was beautiful. I'm sad because I have a problem. Today is my mother's birthday. I wanted to catch a tiger song for her, but then I remembered she loves a bird song best of all. The bird seller doesn't have the kind of bird that I want, and I don't know what to do."

"What kind of bird do you want?" asked the old woman.

"It must be a very special bird," said the little boy.

15

"I know where there is a very special bird,"
said the old woman.
"A golden songbird.
Is that the kind of bird you want?"

"Yes! Yes!" said the little boy.
"That's exactly the kind of bird I want!"

"An old man who lives in a village
beyond the hills has one,"
said the old woman.
"It's a very long way though."

"Can I get there and back before dark?"
asked the little boy.

"Only if you walk very fast,"
replied the old woman.

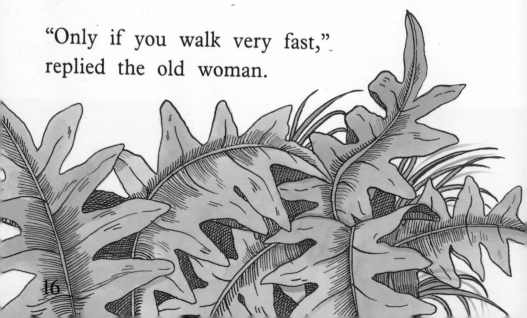

The little boy walked for many hours
in the hot sun.
At last, he reached the village
beyond the hills.
Sure enough, the old man had just the bird
he was looking for.
Its feathers gleamed in the sun,
and its song was like magic.
It cost him all the money he had.
He put the bird under his arm
and set off for home.

The sun was just setting
when the little boy got home.
His mother was very worried indeed.

"Where have you been all day?" she cried.

"Mother," he said, "I have something
for you."

His mother saw that he held something
behind his back.

"Is that your tiger song?" she asked.

"Close your eyes and count to ten,"
the little boy said.
He placed the golden songbird before her.

"That's the most beautiful bird
I've ever seen," said his mother
when she opened her eyes.
"You remembered my birthday after all,
my little boy," she said.
"And all the time, I thought
you had forgotten."

"How could I forget *your* birthday?"
the little boy said.
"I thought of getting you a tiger song,
but then I remembered that you like
a bird song best of all."

That night, when his mother tucked him
into bed, the little boy said,
"You're the best mother
in the whole wide world."

"And you're the best little boy,"
said his mother.
"Now close your eyes and go to sleep."

The little boy fell asleep at once.
All night long, he dreamed beautiful dreams
about lions and golden songbirds
and about the tiger song that he would catch
the next day.